Padma Shri Pran

Maurice Horn, the editor of World Encyclopedia of Comics, has described cartoonist PRAN as Walt Disney of India.

Entertaining generation after generation, his comics have been constant companion of all the growing youngsters providing fun and amusement through his famous characters like CHACHA CHAUDHARY, SABU, SHRIMATIJI, PINKI, BILLOO, RAMAN etc. More than 600 of his titles are selling well in the market, and numerous comic strips are regularly appearing in various newspapers. His CHACHA CHAUDHARY comics had already been adapted for a TV Serial, and ran continuously for 600 episodes on a premier channel.

Travelling widely over the globe, he delivers lectures at various International Conferences. He has also been honoured with 'People of The Year Award' by Limca Book of Records for popularizing comics. His comic book 'United We Stand' was released in 1983 by the then Prime Minister Mrs. Indira Gandhi, and is still very popular among children.

Publisher

4

SOON...

HOW COME MY COMPUTER IS WET?

YOU SAID YOU'VE GOT VIRUS IN THE COMPUTER

SO TO MAKE IT VIRUS FREE, I WASHED IT WITH A SOAP.

GULAB JAMUN

HOW ARE YOU IRAM?

VERY WELL. BUT THIS HOT WEATHER IS UNBEARABLE.

YES, YOU'RE RIGHT. IT IS VERY HOT. TAKE CARE OF YOURSLF.

WEAR LIGHT CLOTHES AND DRINK PLENTY OF WATER.

7

8

9

UNTIMELY RAIN

JHAPATJI...

I FEEL LIKE STROLLING OUT TODAY.

I HAVE TAKEN MY BATH AND AM READY.

I'LL GO.

14

15

HUNGRY UNCLE

I HAVE SAVED MONEY FOR THE PIZZA WITH DIFFICULTY.

TODAY I WILL HAVE MY FILL.

PACK A DOUBLE CHEEZE PIZZA.

I'LL GO HOME AND EAT.

PINKI ALONGWITH THE PIZZA.

HUNGRY UNCLE.

19

CELEBRITY

PINKI!

JHAPAT UNCLE!

WHY ARE YOU STANING HERE?

I AM WAITING FOR THE BUS AS I AM GOING TO THE STAR AUDITORIUM TODAY.

I AM ALSO GOING THERE. SIT.

23

CELEBRITIES.

LET THEM GO.

HOW WAS IT UNCLE JHAPATJI? WONDERFUL.

PAPER LEAK

MUMMY!

WHAT HAPPENED PINKY?

I APPLIED SOAP TO WASH MY FACE.

OH!

BUT THERE'S NO WATER.

DONE.

HERE.

WHENEVER THERE'S ANY LEAKAGE, CALL ME.

PINI AND SNAKE CHARMER

BHIKHU! DOES YOUR PUBLICATION HAVE A JOB FOR ME?

I REQUIRE A PHOTO JOURNALIST FOR MY CHILDREN'S MAGAZINE. DO YOU KNOW PHOTOGRAPHY?

YES! I CAN CLICK PHOTOS.

TAKE THIS! CLICK A UNIQUE PICTURE AND GET A JOB.

I'LL PROVE MYSELF.

32

33

34

35

PINKI
OFF TO SCHOOL

PINKI - ARMY MAN

OHH! THIS CARTOON EPISODE IS A REPEAT TELECAST.

SEEING IT AGAIN IS BORING.

COME, LET'S TAKE A STROLL.

43

44

FIND 10 DIFFERENCES

Find the differences in two Pictures and send us back to win a surprise prize - write down the following details in block letter: Complete Name, Telephone Number with STD code (Mobile Number), Age, Place of Birth, Date of Birth, Gender, Email ID and Complete Postal Address with Pin code.

Discover Talent @ Diamond Toons

X-30, Okhla Industrial Area, Phase-II, New Delhi-110020
Ph.: 011-40712200, E-mail: sales@dpb.in

LET US LEARN
YOGA

Available in Hindi , English, Marathi, Gujarati,Bangla & Odia

Today the whole world is inclined towards Yoga. This is the high time when we can promote Yoga to our children and inculcate its benefits in to them. We have to make them understand about its importance, so that they could become hale & healthy, mentally & physically both.

This book is going to update our children about Yoga, and it would be very easy for them to understand the method of doing each asana.

In this way, they not only will enjoy Yoga, but also going to develop concentration, which in turn help them to achieve big."

Diamond BOOKS
X-30, Okhla Industrial Area Phase-II, New Delhi-110020, Ph.: +91-011-40712200
Email: sales@dpb.in, website:www.diamondbook.in

JOIN THE DOT

Draw a line from dot number 1 to dot number 2, then from dot number 2 to dot number 3, 3 to 4, and so on. Continue to join the dots until you have connected all the numbered dots. Then color the picture!

Join the dot and send us back to win a surprise prize - write down the following details in block letter: Complete Name, Telephone Number with STD code (Mobile Number), Age, Place of Birth, Date of Birth, Gender, Email ID and Complete Postal Address with Pin code.

 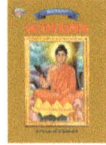